Pursued by the Cowboy

Crossing the Line Series Book 2

By: Alyssa Lee

Copyright 2022 Alyssa Lee

This is a work of fiction. Names, characters, places and incidents are either products of the author's imagination or are used fictitiously. Any similarity to actual events or locales or persons, living or dead, is entirely coincidental.

Free Gift

Sign up to my mailing list and receive this FREE exclusive copy of Her Billionaire Fixated (A prequel to the Heads or Tails series). Also stay up to date with all my new releases, giveaways, contests, cover reveals and more!

To sign up to my newsletter type the following link into your browser https://bookhip.com/ZDPXQQG

Book Description

When Reba Sewell goes out for an afternoon ride, she has no idea what she'll encounter along the way. Upon finding a riderless horse, she investigates – and discovers her childhood enemy, Dirk Blackburn, injured in a ravine. Both the Sewell and Blackburn families have been at war for over a hundred years, and Dirk became a merciless bully to Reba all her life.

She helps him out, and sends him on his way, knowing she'll never see him again, and glad of it. So why does she accept his challenge of a long distance horse race? And why does Reba, who used to be a skinny, introverted girl, intrigue Dirk the way she does? No longer skinny and no longer introverted, she'd blossomed into a self-confident beauty who Dirk cannot resist.

What happens when both of their fathers demand their children forget their love for one another? Read this enemies to lovers and forbidden love romance and find out.

Contents

Chapter One Reba
Chapter Two Dirk
Chapter Three Reba
Chapter Four Dirk
Chapter Five Reba
Chapter Six Dirk
Chapter Seven Reba
Chapter Eight Dirk
Chapter Nine Reba
Chapter Ten Dirk
Other Books by This Author
About The Author

Chapter One

Reba

I loved spring. The fresh, clean air scenting of pine, fir, and evergreen, oaks and elms budding with new life. Robins returned from their winter migration, and very young and small rabbits bolted for cover as my mount's hooves warned them of our approach. High above atop the Bitterroot Mountains, snow gleamed under the bright sunlight.

Khan carried me along the plain dirt road, his neck arched despite the loose rein, his charcoal mane tossing under the light breeze. Curious about the world around us, he looked at the thin forest to either side, his gray ears perked forward. When he came to a sudden and uncharacteristic halt, staring into the woods to our right, I, too, gazed in that direction.

"What?" I asked. "Don't tell me it's a bear, we don't need a hungry bear messing with us."

A short distance away, a horse whinnied. Khan lifted his head, calling back to the stranger.

"Dude, that's Blackburn nag. We don't talk to them. Come on."

I nudged Khan with my heels, and he took an obedient step forward before stopping again, still looking toward the trees and the source of the horse's call. When the big buckskin trotted, clearly lame, from under the pine branches, Khan spun his hindquarters around to face the stranger head-on. Blood streaked the buckskin's left front knee and cannon bone and, while saddled and bridled, the saddle's breast collar had broken. It hung loose by only one strap and the clip attaching it to the cinch.

"Shit," I muttered, swinging down from my saddle.

I led Khan to the barbed wire fence that bordered the Blackburn ranch and separated the buckskin from the road, taking a closer look at the wound. The blood had crusted, and a few flies buzzed around it, informing me that the horse had gotten hurt an hour or so ago. So where's the saddle's occupant?

"Where's your rider?" I asked, grabbing his bridle over the fence. "Is someone hurt back there?"

The gelding touched noses with Khan, introducing himself. "You're a Blackburn, knot head, you'd better not give my horse cooties."

Indecisive, I stared beyond him to the forest and pastures belonging to the Blackburn clan. If the rider had fallen off, which I felt certain he or she had, I felt obligated to go help. But helping meant cutting the wire fence to get Khan through, and that was against the law. So was trespassing. Nor would I leave my horse alone while I walked in.

"Maybe I should just call 911," I muttered. "But what if that person dies while I dither? Jeez, just go already."

Leaving the two horses to decide who was bigger and badder, I dug into my saddlebags for my wire cutters. After cutting all four strands, I pulled the heavy wire back while holding onto the buckskin. I certainly didn't need him disappearing down the road where he might get hurt. His reins in my hand, I remounted Khan, then nudged him in the direction from which the buckskin had come.

"Hello?" I called, riding at a walk with the buckskin's head at my knee. Fortunately, he ambled quietly at Khan's side without acting up. Surprising, given his origins on the Blackburn ranch.

"Hello? Can anyone hear me?"

I heard nothing except the crunch of hooves on dead leaves and pine needles, the sound of birds flitting amid the branches above us. No yells for help, no calls of *I'm over here.* Dread that I'd find a dead body or the rider seriously injured seeped into me. I'd forgotten all the first aid I'd learned in high school.

"Anyone out here?"

"Yeah."

The male voice sounded faint yet clear enough I could follow the sound. "Keep yelling."

"I'm in the ravine, down here."

"Are you alright?"

"I think I busted my ankle."

At least I won't have to perform CPR. Not that I remember how, anyway. A few hundred yards ahead, I found the ravine. Its edge jumbled with rocks, boulders, long-dead trees, it sloped steeply downward. I dismounted and tied both horses to a sturdy oak branch, then worked my way amid the treacherous rim to peer down and past a big boulder.

A cowboy in a black Stetson, jeans, boots, and a gray t-shirt sat on a rock at the ravine's bottom, his mouth twisted in pain. At catching my movement, he looked up. His eyes widened with something I couldn't quite identify. Incredulity?

"Reba?"

"Oh, the joy is mine."

I, too, sat on a rock, making myself comfortable and gazing down at the man who'd made it his life's work to make mine miserable. I took off my hat and my sunglasses, then swiped a few tendrils of hair back from my eyes. With easy deliberation, I put them both back on and glanced around the ravine he was stuck in.

"You got yourself into quite a fix, Blackburn," I drawled.

He grimaced, his tanned face growing dark with either anger or humiliation. I could see blood caked on it and a few places where is had already swelled. *He must really have taken a mighty tumble.*

"My horse tripped and fell, dammit, tossed me over the edge."

"You never could ride worth a damn," I remarked. "Your nag must have curvature of the spine from lugging both you and your ego around."

He shoved his hat back on his head, revealing more of his thick, night-black hair, his brilliant blue eyes a sharp contrast to his tanned skin. Had I not hated him since infancy, I'd appreciate his powerful good looks, his chiseled features, even his tight ass in his jeans.

"If you're not going to help me, can you at least call someone who will?"

"Why would I do that? I kinda like seeing you under my boots."

"I busted my cell when I tumbled down here." He took his hat off and wiped sweat from his brow before replacing it. Though the temperature could be considered warm, it certainly wasn't hot enough to sweat. *Maybe he's in a lot of pain. Good.*

"Did you find my horse?" he asked, shifting uncomfortably. He lifted his right leg, revealing his torn jeans from the knee down. Other portions of his broad, muscular chest and shoulders displayed rips and tears in both his shirt and his skin.

"Is that what you call it?" I inquired politely. "I thought it looked like a mutated camel."

He drew in a strong breath. "Please, Reba. Will you help me get out of here?"

"Begging now?" I smirked. "I like it. After all the times you made me cry, I now get to witness you in tears."

"I'm not crying."

"I bet you will when I simply ride away."

"If I apologize for tormenting you when we were kids, will that help?"

"Nope. Time has long past for apologies. You were an asshole then, Dirk, and you're an asshole now."

He lowered his head, his face hidden by his Stetson, but I thought I saw his jaw tighten.

"I certainly can't make up for the past right now," he said. "All I can say is that I've changed since you saw me last."

"Oh, please," I snorted. "You'll never change."

He lifted his head to scowl up at me. "Nor will you. You were a stone-cold bitch in high school, and it's obvious you still are."

"Oh, appealing to the humanity in me?" I smiled warmly. "That'll get you out of that ravine real quick. How long before your clan realizes you haven't returned home? Tonight? Tomorrow? Do they even know, in this vast wilderness, where the hell you are?"

Dirk Blackburn turned his tense face away. "My folks won't be back until Saturday. The hands won't miss me at all."

I almost felt pity for him. Almost. "So that leaves me, I reckon. I could fetch a rope and drag your useless ass out of there."

"Or just call 911. Tell them where I am."

I eyed the steep walls of the ravine, the jagged rocks on both sides, the barkless, dead trunks tossed among them from some long ago flood. What I didn't see was a gentler slope whereby I could take the horses down into the ravine, boost him onto his nag, and let him ride out. Even if there had been, I wouldn't have risked Khan's legs amid the sharp rocks on the old riverbed.

"Can you put any weight on that foot?"

Dirk eased his way to a standing position, showing me more blood on his shirt over his back and hips. There was deep bruising on his muscular arms I hadn't seen before.

"Not very well."

"Look, I'll throw a rope down to you," I said, standing. "I'll tie it to my horse and with the support, you can limp up the side, right?"

"Yeah, I think so."

I untied Khan from the tree and led him to the ravine. Taking my lariat, I shook out the loop, then tossed it to Dirk. It barely reached him. Still, he slid his arms through the loop, then took hold of it and nodded his readiness.

"Take it slow, okay?"

"Don't tell me what to do, Blackburn."

I tied the rope's end to my saddle horn, then called out, "I'm taking up the slack."

"Gotcha."

My hand on Khan's bridle, I encouraged him to walk a few paces. The rope tightened, and Dirk yelled, "Slow, dammit."

"Whoa."

Leaving Khan to stand, I peered over the edge. Dirk, crouched on the rocks, was crawling upward, dragging his busted right leg as the rope's loop cut into his chest. Turning his pain-racked face toward me, he gave me a quick thumbs up. "I'm good."

"I'll dispute that later."

Step by step, Khan slowly hauled Dirk up from the ravine's depths. Fortunately, while steep, the side itself was only about fifty feet. At the top, he caught hold of a half-buried rock and hauled himself hand over hand to lie, gasping and sweating, on the stony ground.

I backed Khan to put slack in the rope and untied it from the horn. Walking back to Dirk, Khan at my shoulder, I looked down at him.

"You're a mess."

He chuckled, still gasping for breath. "Thanks."

"It wasn't a compliment."

"Of course not. No Blackburn would ever get a compliment from a Sewell."

He sat up slowly, wincing, and pulled the rope from around his chest. Halfway up, he paused, staring at my horse.

"What the hell is that? A rat with a saddle?"

Far too used to his insults to be offended, I smiled. "He's a horse far better than your brain-dead nag. And he pulled your ass out, remember?"

Dirk finished the journey to his feet. Bleeding, filthy, and sexy as hell, he put weight on his left leg only.

"Arabians aren't cow horses."

"He can out-work, and out-cow your quarter horse."

"That, you'll have to prove."

"I don't have to prove anything, dirtbag," I snapped. "Now, I'm outta here."

I started to put my foot in my stirrup and mount, but Dirk's extended hand stopped me.

"Reba, please, sorry about that. I can't get on my horse without some help."

Rolling my eyes, I glanced over my shoulder at the patient buckskin.

"Jeez, I have to do everything for you."

"I really appreciate what you're doing."

"Yeah, sure you do." Turning my back, I stalked to the horse and untied his reins. "You lamed him pretty good."

Dirk's face was stricken as I led his gelding to him, his blue eyes on the badly scraped foreleg.

"Oh, man."

"You shouldn't be riding him."

"I don't have much choice." He cocked his eye at me, a small grin tugging his mouth. "Unless I can ride your rat."

"Like hell you will," I retorted. "You aren't worthy to ride Khan."

After I jerry-rigged the breast collar, I tossed the reins over the gelding's neck and held his bridle as Dirk slowly and painfully climbed his way onto a rock. From there, he scrambled awkwardly, wincing and cussing, into the wide saddle. Breathing hard, he leaned down to put his left boot in the stirrup, his useless right simply dangling.

"I owe you, Reba," he said quietly, picking up his reins. "I always pay my debts."

"Pay me back by staying the hell away from me."

I swung into my own saddle, then reined Khan around.

"You gonna repair that hole in the fence you made?" he called after me as I walked Khan toward the road.

For answer, I flipped him the single finger salute over my shoulder without turning in my saddle. I heard his laugh from behind me.

Yeah, I fixed the fence. I didn't want to, but ranching was in my blood, and broken fences needed mending.

No matter whose fence it was.

Chapter Two

Dirk

Listless and stoned on Vicodin, I stared at the wide-screen, flat panel television, vacantly watching whatever show my remote landed on. My lower right leg, encased in a rubber boot meant for icing a horse's leg, currently held enough ice to give me frostbite. Though I felt certain I'd busted the ankle, the emergency room quacks had diagnosed a bad sprain. From my knee on down, I didn't have a leg.

Instead, I had a swollen and badly bruised appendage incapable of bearing my weight.

"I have way too much work to be laid up," I muttered, my tongue thick from the dope.

From the floor beside my chair, Magnum lifted his muzzle to gaze up at me, perhaps thinking I'd spoken to him. A Belgian Malinois, attack trained and my closest companion, he uttered a small woof, perhaps asking me a question.

"Never mind. Just talking to myself."

I heard a door open and slam shut from down the front hall.

"Hey, Dirty Dirk, where you at, son?"

"In here."

Magnum, recognizing my visitor, rose to his paws, stretched, then ambled toward the door. Heavy boots, most likely covered in mud, tromped in my direction. Jimmy's cheerful grin faded as he gaped from my den's doorway.

"Holy hounds of hell," he breathed. "What happened to you?" Bending, he rubbed Magnum's ears in rough affection.

"You know that deep ravine on the west side, not far from the road?"

"Yeah."

"It happened."

Jimmy, my best friend since kindergarten, and a man I swore could ride Pegasus himself and never get thrown, sat on the love seat not far from my recliner, muddy boots and all. Reddish blond hair and a smattering of freckles, Jimmy was built like a Sherman tank. All muscle and bone, yet with a sharp mind and quick wit. His hazel eyes took in the boot.

"What's in there?"

"Ice and pain."

"How long you had ice in there with your pain?"

I glanced at the fake antique wall clock. "Nearly an hour."

"Great jumpin' Josephat," he bellowed, rising with a scowl. "You want to keep your leg?"

"It isn't doing me much good now, is it?"

Bending over my useless appendage as it rested on a pillow on the coffee table, Jimmy lifted it carefully, then gently eased the long boot off. Ice and water splashed on the table and my carpet as he set it aside, staring in awe. Five times its normal size, blackened and scraped, my ankle was wrapped in a soaked Ace bandage. My leg looked more like an overcooked sausage than a leg.

"What have you done, child?"

Numb from the knee down, I hardly felt his touch as he unwrapped the soggy bandage.

"Barney shied," I murmured, "stumbled, went down. I went straight off and down the embankment."

Jimmy examined my badly swollen and bruised ankle. "You'll be lucky if this heals right, man."

"The docs say it will. Not broken, just needs ice and rest."

"So how'd you get out of the ravine?" he asked, shaking his head as he sat back down.

"You won't believe it."

"Try me. No, wait. You got any beer?"

"In the fridge. Bring me one."

While alcohol and Vicodin weren't exactly a great cocktail, I didn't care. Since returning to the ranch and my house, on crutches, I hadn't been able to keep Reba Sewell out of my mind. In middle school, she was a knock-kneed filly with braces, and a fine target for bullying. In high school, she's lost the braces, her knees straightened, but she remained shy, reserved, awkward, and again, a fine target for bullying.

The self-confident, blonde bombshell in tight jeans, a blue tank top, dark shades, and a straw cowboy hat with feathers who had looked down at me with contempt seemed almost like a stranger. She had curves and boobs and an ass that could make a man mad with lust. I could fall in love.

Except she hated my guts.

"So tell," Jimmy said, handing me a bottle of Shiner Bock. Magnum returned to his spot beside my chair and lay down with a grunt and a sigh.

"Spill it. Did you crawl out?"

"Sort of." I took a long swallow. "But I had help."

"Oooh, the suspense."

"Reba Sewell."

Jimmy's bottle halted halfway between his chest and his mouth. For a moment, his eyes went blank as he put a face to the name. Then he choked.

"Reba? You're kidding."

"Nope. I reckon she was riding by and found Barney. Knew there was trouble and came looking. You know that girl was riding an Arabian?"

"Contrary to your prejudices," Jimmy commented, relaxing, "Arabs make fine ranch horses."

"You know damn well they don't have the sense God gave a sheep. Always spooking, you can't rope off them, they don't have the speed."

"Forget the horse. Tell me about Reba."

I took a long swallow, remembering her supermodel beauty, her flawless skin, the way she moved with grace, how well she sat in the saddle.

"Stunning."

"Yeah? I always thought she was cute." Jimmy chuckled. "In a sweet, innocent sort of way."

"I guess she was," I agreed reluctantly. "But couldn't say boo to a mouse. Always cold toward me... distant, like I was scum."

"Uh, dude?" Jimmy waved his bottle. "I hate to break it to you, but you *were* scum. Hot football player, always had a cheerleader or three hanging on you, looked down your nose on us mere mortals."

I stared at him. "I didn't do that to you."

"No, because I'd put you on your ass if you tried." Jimmy smirked. "But to kids like Reba and her ilk, you trashed them every moment you could get."

"Thanks for making me feel like a small pile of dog shit."

"You're welcome."

I drank my beer in sullen silence, trying to recall exactly what it felt like to bully kids who were smaller, younger, and frightened of me and my friends. It seemed like a lifetime ago, as the years between then and now had changed me. War seemed to do that.

"Now Reba despises me."

"So?"

I scowled over my Shiner Bock. "She's gorgeous, self-confident, tough as nails, and you know damn well that's the sort that attracts me."

Jimmy laughed. "Your family and hers have been at each other's throats for what? Three generations? Four?"

"Four," I grumbled. "Our great-grandfathers started the feud before the turn of the century."

"I can see it now." Jimmy chuckled. "'Mom, Dad, meet my new girlfriend, Reba. Oh, yeah, she's a Sewell, but that doesn't matter.' Son, your old man will gut you, skin you, and hang your hide on the barn wall if you date her."

"Don't you get it, dummy?" I yelled, sparking fresh pain from my leg and bringing Magnum up with raised hackles, "that girl saved my ass. If she hadn't come by, I'd still be in that damn ravine. I owe her, big time. And if I try to pay my debt, *she'll* hang my hide on the barn wall."

"If she won't accept you trying to pay it, then drop it. Easy peasy."

I groaned. "That's not how it works. Afghanistan taught me that."

Magnum rested his head on my healthy left knee, his soulful brown eyes on my face. I stroked his fur and his soft ears, thinking of what I owed this mutt and how I couldn't ever repay him for saving my life. Nor would he understand if I tried. All he wanted from me was love, loyalty, and a decent roof over his head. Food once in a while, I reckoned.

"Look, there isn't much you can do," Jimmy commented. "Just drop it. That hairy beastie wasn't with you, right? No way could any beautiful chica get near you with him around."

"I had to make him stay home," I murmured, still stroking his head. "He cut his paw on something, and I didn't want him on it, maybe getting it infected."

"Ah. How's he doing?"

"Unlike me, he's not on crutches. And unlike me, he'll heal quickly."

Jimmy drank from his bottle, grimacing as he swallowed. "That leg is a horror. You'll be off it for a month."

"I can't afford to be off it a month," I griped, sending Magnum back to the floor with a snap of my fingers. "I have Dad's new colts to break, calves to brand. He's counting on me."

"Maybe he'll hire me to replace you."

I choked on my beer. "Are you out of a job *again*?"

"Yup. Old man Tyson didn't like me fooling around with his daughter. Man, that girl has tentacles. When she wants it, she *wants* it."

"You're as randy as a billy goat."

Jimmy grinned. "And proud of it."

Huffing a sigh, I considered. "Yeah, he'll hire you. He always did like you, though I can't imagine why."

"It's my charm and incredible good looks."

"It's because you can ride anything with hair."

"That, too."

I upended my bottle only to discover it had no beer in it.

"Get us another, will you?"

"Are you on drugs?" he demanded.

"Vicodin."

"Oh, that and beer will mess you up real good. Your dad will adopt me after your funeral." Jimmy stood and ambled into my kitchen where I heard him open my fridge. "You have only two left."

"That's cool."

"Where are your folks, by the way?" he asked, handing me a fresh bottle.

"Went to Billings," I answered, popping the cap off. "My granddaddy isn't doing well. Cancer."

"He the one who started the feud with the Sewells?"

"No, this is my mom's dad. That great-granddaddy died a long time ago, and my dad's daddy is still kicking up dust, yelling how we need to hunt down every last Sewell and take their land."

"Ah. The state of Montana don't take kindly to murder and land grabbing these days."

"Try telling *him* that," I groused, taking a drink. "He still thinks its 1945 and Rupert Sewell is stealing his cattle."

Jimmy barked laughter. "How old is that coot?"

"Shit." I had to think. "In his nineties, anyway. Can't remember."

"So Rupert Sewell is Reba's... what? Granddad?"

I frowned. "Yeah."

"How'd that feud start, anyway? You probably told me, but I forgot."

"My great-granddad and the Sewell ancestor started out as neighbors and friends," I replied, feeling pain return to my right leg. "But Sewell blamed my granddad for a fire that burned his barn and killed some valuable horses. It seems a Sewell, the arsonist, left evidence behind. Anyway, each family continued to cut fences, stealing cattle and horses from each other. By the 70s, that came to a stop, but both families still despise and hate each other."

"The Hatfields and the McCoys," Jimmy commented.

"Not quite that bad, but almost. Blackburns and Sewells didn't actually murder one another, but it came close." I sighed. "And I just had to bully the latest of the Sewell scions in school only to have her save my ass. What irony."

"Could be worse." Jimmy drank his beer.

"How so?"

"She could have left your ass in that ravine."

"Yeah. She could've. She didn't. I wonder why?"

"Because deep down she's a decent human being?"

"God." I groaned. "Don't tell my parents that."

Chapter Three

Reba

"You should have left him to rot."

So said my illustrious sire at the supper table. Rupert Sewell Jr. was brought up to despise all Blackburns and had passed some of that prejudice on to me as I grew up. However, much of my hatred for Dirk Blackburn came from how he and his friends had treated me. As for his parents, or his ancestors, I couldn't give a rat's ass either way.

"It gets awful cold at night," I replied, forking Mom's noodle casserole into my mouth. "Besides, it was the right thing to do."

Dad snorted, glowering. "He wouldn't have frozen to death, it ain't that cold. So what if he suffered through a chilly night? Why should we care?"

"She's right," Mom, Brigitte, interjected. "We raised her to be conscientious and caring. I for one would be disappointed if she had walked away from the boy."

I laughed. "He's not much of a boy now, Mom. He's all man. And a real hunk."

Dad glared as though I'd spoken a dirty word. "Dirk Blackburn is just like the rest of that clan. You can't trust him as far as you can spit him. He'll stab you in the back, right enough. Just stay away from him, you hear?"

"Why would I want to have anything to do with him, Dad?" I demanded. "He bullied me in school. Jeez, I'm lucky I didn't commit suicide the way some kids do these days."

"Reba!" My mom dropped her fork into her casserole. "You never told us you were bullied in school. Why didn't you?"

"This is the first I've heard of that going on in this town," Dad added. "You sure about that? It wasn't normal teasing?"

"I think I can tell the difference between bullying and teasing," I replied, annoyed. "And what could anyone do about it? Informing you guys or the school would accomplish nothing, and maybe make it worse."

"We could have tried," Brigitte said, upset. "Talked to the school board, demand they intervene and stop it. Teachers can't be allowed to ignore this behavior."

"They do, Mom," I told her. "Much easier to not get involved."

"How long did this go on?"

"First grade through high school graduation."

"We should sue them," Rupert grumbled. "Take 'em to court. Sue 'em for every penny they have and will have in the future."

"I can't believe you never told us this," Brigitte exclaimed as though I'd hidden a terrible secret from her. Okay, so maybe I did. No one could have stopped Dirk and his chums anyway—they'd have simply become more discreet.

"Sorry."

"She's a tough kid," Dad added. "She turned out all right. Isn't in one of those insane asylums."

"That's not the point, Rupert," Mom snapped. "We weren't there for our daughter when she needed us."

"If she needed us, then she'd have told us what was going on, right?" Rupert continued to glare and included Brigitte in his irritation. "It's not much surprising that a Blackburn kid would turn out rotten, pick on a small girl. His crazy old man probably put him up to it."

"He said he's changed," I mused, taking a drink from my tea. "Wanted to apologize for how he behaved."

"Sure. Because he needed your help."

"Says he owes me a debt."

Rupert jabbed his index finger at me. "You stay away from that boy, understand? He's bad, he's trouble, and he'll bring nothing but trouble on you."

"You treat me as though I'm a little kid," I protested, pissed. "I'm not. And I'm only living here because you need me to help run this ranch."

"What? You want to move out?"

"Not necessarily, but I might if you keep nagging on me."

Dad opened his mouth to berate me further, but Mom intercepted his tirade before it started.

"Stop it," she snapped. "Reba already said she doesn't like him. There's no need to keep bellowing about the Blackburns. Besides, maybe she doesn't want to be a part of this damn feud. You and Billy Blackburn are the ones who keep it alive. Maybe it's time for the next generation to bury the hatchet."

Rupert gaped as though she'd spoken blasphemy. In his mind, perhaps she had.

"I can't believe you'd say such a thing. That clan is no good, full of thieves and back-stabbers. And I have no intention of letting my daughter become even remotely friendly with any of them." His cutting glare caught me within its sights. "You understand me?"

I sighed dramatically. "Loud and clear, jeez."

"I don't appreciate your tone, missy."

The word *duh* rose to the front of my mind, but I swallowed it before letting it slip out. Under normal circumstances, Rupert was a decent enough guy and father, humorous and generous. Yet, on the subject of the Blackburn clan, he tended to lose his mind. And, no, I didn't want to be drawn into the Sewell-Blackburn feud or raise any future kids to despise people who hadn't done anything to them.

A jerk of the first order, Dirk would never be my first choice as a friend, or even an acquaintance. Still, I recalled that his brilliant blue eyes had failed to hold that look I'd learned to fear in school. That mean light, that malicious glee when he planned to push me into my locker and click the lock shut.

As I finished my dinner in silence, I thought about his Adonis-like good looks, his expression of shock upon seeing me for the first time since graduation, his pleasant half-smile when he said he owed me a debt. He hadn't treated me with the same callous disdain he always had while we were young.

Because he needed you. He hasn't changed. Not one iota. Stay the hell away from him.

***

"Dirk Blackburn?" Marsha, my best friend since middle school, exclaimed in my ear through the phone. "Oh my God, he's gorgeous. I ran into him at the coffee shop."

"What was he like?" I asked, lying on the same bed my parents had bought me when I turned ten. "Was he nice, I mean?"

"Oh, yeah. Gave me a hug, said he was glad to see me. You know he joined the army after graduation."

"I never heard that."

"Oh, yeah. His best friend is my brother-in-law, remember? Told me a few things about Dirk over the years. I didn't tell you because of how much you hated him."

"So did you," I protested. "He treated you like shit, too, you know. Dirk and Jimmy and all the others."

"I know. But when I married Jake, Jimmy turned around. He's a really nice guy, though kind of a womanizer."

"I've heard that in town." I stared thoughtfully at my ceiling. "I helped Dirk today."

"Doing what?"

"He took a bad tumble into a ravine on his family ranch. Busted him up a bit. Khan and I pulled him out."

"Oooh, so that's where this line of questioning is going. That was good of you to do it, given your past with him. Dirk picked on you most among all of us."

"Because our families hate each other."

"Yeah, that long-running feud. So was Dirk nasty even though you helped him?"

"No. He tried to be sweet, but I shut him down."

"I guess I can't blame you."

"He said he'd changed since high school."

"Well," Marsha said slowly, "he *did* fight in Afghanistan, according to Jimmy. I can see that happening after being in the middle of that meat grinder."

"Yeah, maybe."

"So?"

"So what?"

"You gonna try to see him?"

I rolled my eyes. "You know better than that, Marsh. He's a dead-end loser."

She chuckled. "He's sexier than Thor."

"Good looks don't equate to a good heart."

"You'd know all about that, after what Doug put you through."

"Oh, yeah." I recalled the last time I saw Doug, madder than a bull with a broken pecker. I'd told him our relationship was toast, to stop calling and texting me, and to hit the road. He didn't take that advice well at *all*. "That yo-yo still texts me once in a while. Trying to weasel back in."

"You aren't going to let him, right?" Marsha's alarmed voice rose a few decibels.

"Of course not, chill out. Dating him for six months was six months too long. He sure can dance, though."

"The real question is, however," Marsha's voice turned sly, "was he good in bed?"

"As I have so few comparisons," I replied, "I'd have to say he was just okay. Only interested in getting himself off."

"I'm so very lucky Jake is a terrific lover. Always puts my pleasure first."

"That's rare, baby."

"I know it. One day you'll snag a guy like that."

"I strongly suspect you snagged the last one. The only other considerate lovers are gay."

"Want me to get the skinny on Dirk?"

"And what skinny would that be? That he works out, can't ride for shit? That he's working on his parents' ranch? I really don't care."

"I'll get the intel on him and call you tomorrow."

"Hey," I began, but she'd already hung up.

***

The next day, I answered Marsha's call on the second ring.

"Jimmy says Dirk really has changed," Marsha said eagerly. "He has some PTSD, brought home a real war dog from the war. And he's a decorated hero, did some real badass shit over there, saved a bunch of lives."

"And I'm supposed to care why?" I asked tiredly, my phone to my ear as I brushed Khan's dapple-gray coat. "I'm not interested, Marsha. Doug turned me off to men for a long time, and if Blackburn was the last man on earth, I'd still tell him to kiss my ass."

"Jimmy says Dirk could fall in love with you."

I dropped my phone into the barn floor dirt. Khan eyed me with concern, his huge brown eyes focused on me as I hastily bent to pick up my cell only to drop the brush in the same place. Marsha's voice squeaked from the speaker as I wiped the dirt from the screen.

"Sorry, I dropped my phone," I said, my mouth dry. "And I don't believe a word you're saying."

She giggled. "Believe it. Jimmy would know."

"Uh, no. I flipped him off, told him to stay out of my life, there's no way on this green planet that scrotum boil could ever fall in love with me."

"Scrotum boil?"

"Nor me with him. Nuh uh, Jimmy's talking shit, telling lies he'll burn in hell for."

"Scrotum boil?"

"Must I explain?"

"My, honey, you have quite the vocabulary."

"Be quiet or I'll use it on you. Now I have to go. Khan's giving me the stink eye because I haven't scratched his itchy spots."

"You'll never love a man the way you love that horse."

"No man could ever measure up to him. Now quit getting info from Jimmy."

"Later, honey."

***

Over the next month, as spring moved closer to hotter summer, I actually managed to forget about Dirk and pulling him from the ravine. Marsha finally stopped nagging me about him. As a coordinator for the town's gymkhana club, I rode Khan amidst the kids, preteens, and teenagers who were riding, saddling, and grooming their mounts for the competitions to come. I reined in, frowning at a trio of girls in jeans, boots, and long-sleeved shirts with their numbers already pinned to their backs.

Standing by their saddled and patiently tied horses, it became clear they intended to go full-out in some down and dirty fighting. I reined Khan toward them and caught their attention the instant his shadow loomed over them. The three girls gaped up at us, their fight forgotten.

"Ladies," I said agreeably, "you know the club's rules. No fighting. Keep it up, and you'll take your horses home right now."

"Yes, ma'am," said one, who then untied her palomino from the trailer.

"Yes, ma'am," chimed in the other two, who also turned away from one another to collect their mounts.

I reined Khan around in a tight spin off his rear quarters and halted in shock.

Dirk Blackburn, mounted on his buckskin gelding only a horse's length away, thumbed his hat back and grinned at me.

"Hi, Reba."

Chapter Four

Dirk

Reba's peaches and cream, sexier than sin itself and the perfect image of a cowgirl, was exactly as I remembered her. She wore the same shades, her hat pulled down low over her forehead. Instead of a tank top, she wore a silver long-sleeved Western shirt, a gold belt buckle she no doubt earned in her younger years, jeans, and boots. Her golden hair hung in a tight braid over her shoulder and across her right breast.

I leaned my arm on my saddle horn, grinning at her inability to tell me to go fuck myself.

"How are you?" I asked. "You look good."

"I'm all right." She spoke stiffly, neither friendly nor unfriendly. "You? How's your leg?"

I kicked my right boot free of my stirrup and flexed it at my knee. "It's still swollen in places, gets sore if I do too much."

"Was it broken?"

"Naw. Badly sprained."

"I suppose that's better than breaking an ankle."

I glanced around at the teeming throng of horses, kids, their parents, and judges who had all gathered at the county fairgrounds for the weekend's gymkhana festivities. I remembered riding my first horse at one of these when I was maybe six years old.

"You're a part of this shindig? I saw you break up the fight."

"Yeah, I help coordinate the events, find the judges, manage the entries."

Her face lowered, but as she was half-hidden behind her shades and hat, I couldn't tell what she was looking for.

"He healed up well. Hardly a scar."

"Yeah," I agreed. "We were both off work for a long time. We have a Mexican dude who works for us. He's an artist at healing horses. Great guy."

As I spoke, I eyed her Arab. His neck arched with the typical Arabian high set neck, easily as quiet as Barney. His ears indicated he awaited his rider's next order, the sign of a well-trained mount. His curved, dished face and the wide nostrils of his desert ancestors offended me, however, for how could any decent horse breathe through such a deep dish?

"Thanks for fixing the fence."

Reba inclined her head. "Gotta go. Nice chatting."

She reined the dappled-gray around me, but I turned Barney to ride alongside her. Reba sent me a tight-mouthed, crusty look that I simply ignored.

"Great weather for this," I commented lightly.

"What are you doing here?" she demanded.

"I used to ride in this club," I replied, gazing around, "way back when. Barrels, pole bending, showmanship, Western pleasure. Had a great horse. My first. A short little sorrel. But he was fast, quick. I came off him because he ran straight out from under me." I grinned. "I loved that horse."

"Landed on your head, did you?" Reba asked, her tone arched.

"Oh, sure," I answered, agreeable. "And my ass, and my belly, and my back. So why do you ride that Arab?"

"Why not?" she replied. "Arabs are known for their intelligence, loyalty, stamina, they have as much cow sense as quarters, can turn on a dime and give you change. Did you know Arabians have won cutting horse championships?"

"I never heard that," I admitted.

"You should look outside your self-centeredness once in a while."

"I saw tough little desert horses in Afghanistan," I said thoughtfully. "Could carry a man across the mountains on only a little water and feed. I have to admit they impressed me."

Reba caressed the gray's neck under its thick mane. "I raised Khan from a foal," she said, her tone softer than I'd ever heard it. "Registered purebred from some of the oldest lines in Egypt. I only gelded him because my dad forced me to."

"This isn't exactly Arab country."

"Arabs are everywhere," Reba scoffed. "If you watch today, you'll see tons of Arabs and half-Arabs competing. And winning. I suppose you also didn't know that by breeding to an Arabian, you improve whatever breed you bred to."

"So says you," I snorted.

"So says all the experts." She grinned. "Even dead-brained quarter horse people."

I nudged Barney into a trot and reined him in front of her, effectively halting Reba's forward progress.

"I'll make you a bet."

"What bet?"

"You and I race. From Dead Man's Creek all the way to the interstate."

Reba gaped. "That's what, twenty-five miles?"

"Twenty-six, actually. We start at sunrise tomorrow. We'll bring a pair of fair judges to witness it."

"And what does the winner get?"

"I win, you have dinner with me."

"And if I win?"

I shrugged lazily, grinning. "You name your prize."

Reba smiled slowly. "How about your horse?"

"Okay, bad idea. Um, what do you want if you win?"

Her smile didn't change. "I'll let you know."

"Not my horse."

"Not your horse, agreed. Can your leg hold up?" She still smiled that mysterious smile.

"I sure hope so. Because I plan to win that race."

***

With Jimmy yawning in his truck as a judge, I sat aboard Barney and watched the sun rise over the eastern horizon. The year-round snow on the tall peaks glowed pink and purple, the early sun itself peeking over the earth's rim. A truck moved down the dirt road toward us, pulling a horse trailer behind it.

"There she is," Jimmy said, his boots hanging out the window as he lounged across the seat.

"Who's her judge?"

"Marsha, my sister-in-law."

"Shit," I grumbled. "I'll have to wait while Reba saddles her rat."

"Son, you asked for more trouble than you need," Jimmy drawled. "No way can your fat crowbait win this thing."

"Eat me."

"Whip it out, son."

The old Ford and trailer wheezed to a dusty halt beside my truck and four-horse, slant load rig. Reba hopped out from the driver's side and, without acknowledging my presence, went around to the trailer's back. Opening the rear door, she dropped the heavy ramp.

"C'mon, let's go," she ordered.

Fully saddled and bridled, the dappled-gray backed down the ramp, then stood quiet, gazing around. Jimmy sat up and took a long look.

"I wish my horse would do that," he muttered. "Jeez, I have to about drag him out of a trailer."

Reba sure knows how to train a horse. "You ready, Mizz Sewell?"

As her rat stood, his reins on his neck, Reba tightened her cinch.

"Are you ready to eat my dust?"

I chuckled. "It'll be you eating mine."

After I tightened my cinch and swung into my saddle, both Jimmy and Marsha stood ready and waiting. Reba, mounted, her shades on, her hat pulled low, walked the rat to stand beside me. We exchanged a long look, then she smiled.

"It'll be a hot one today," she mused, pulling her hat down firmly on her head.

I did the same. "Yep. I'll be around to help bury your rat."

Her smile deepened, then she faced forward.

Jimmy and Marsha stepped out of the way, their hands in the air. Then both dropped them in a flash.

I kicked Barney into a fast gallop, the starting speed that made the quarter horse famous. Leaning forward over his withers, I encouraged him to run hard, run fast, and get to the interstate long before Reba and her saddle rat. Shooting a quick glance over my shoulder, I saw nothing of her. Or her rat.

I whooped, triumphant. I had the race in the bag already. *Dinner with Reba, here we come.*

An hour later, lathered, his head low, Barney trotted along the dirt road where cars seldom passed. This was a ranch road, used by ranchers and their visitors, and wasn't on any road map. As Reba predicted, the sun bore down on my hat and Barney's head like molten steel. I slowed his trot to a walk to give him a breather.

Suspecting we'd come only about five miles, I glanced back over my shoulder. There they were, trotting along at a fashionable pace, hardly hurrying. *Dammit.* I kicked Barney back into a jog, determined to stay ahead of that rat and his rider. *No wonder the Sewells are dirt farmers. No damn sense.*

Pushing Barney as hard as I dared, having left Reba far behind, I slowed him to a walk. His head low and nostrils flaring, Barney ambled along the dirt road while lather foamed on his neck and chest. Halting, I dismounted. I'd packed in my saddlebags a fold-up plastic waterer and a jug of water.

Barney drank gratefully as I rested my sore right leg. I'd pushed it too hard but promised myself a good rest after I won this race. Leaning against my saddle, I took my hat off to wipe sweat from my brow and my eyes. Damn, it got hot fast.

I never heard her coming.

Reba reined in, removing her sunglasses to study not me but Barney.

"He's not looking too good, Blackburn. You don't want to ruin him."

Fuck me. Her damn rat had hardly raised a sweat. His neck was damp, sure, but not a speck of lather touched his neck, chest, or even dripped from under the saddle. Shit, his nostrils weren't even flared.

"Mind your own business."

Reba shrugged. "Whatever."

I didn't see her leg move, but the Arab picked up the lope from a standstill. Within a minute, they'd rounded a bend in the road to vanish from my sight. Cussing under my breath, I packed up the water into my saddlebags, then mounted. Fresher after water and rest, Barney cantered along easily for a time.

But I couldn't catch up to Reba.

"Where the hell is she?" I muttered, unable to see her ahead of us.

If she'd continued to trot, I should have seen her. I didn't even see the dust from her passage. The sun crossed the sky above us, hot and intense, making both Barney and me sweat heavily. Once again, I halted to give him water and rest before riding on. *Where is she?*

In the trucks, Jimmy and Marsha would be waiting for us at the interstate where the dirt road ended, ready to declare the winner. The afternoon wore on while Barney started to lag. A trot was no longer an option, and a canter absolutely impossible if I wanted to keep him alive. I dismounted and walked him, trudging along the road, sweat running down my face in rivers.

How long have we been at this? I glanced at my cell. Nearly three in the afternoon. My right leg ached fiercely, forcing me to limp, yet I needed to give Barney a decent rest. Only when it threatened to give out completely did I reluctantly mount again. Instead of putting my right boot in the stirrup, I let it hang, loose and limp.

The distant roar of traffic on the interstate reached my ears. Barney's head, low enough to reach his chest, bobbed listlessly up and down with every step. I, too, sagged in the saddle, thirsty and feeling as dried out and empty as a corn husk. Did Reba fall by the wayside and I just didn't see her? I had to have passed her by. Maybe she'd quit and turned back.

Up ahead, I saw the trucks, unmistakable with their trailers. The cooler I'd packed that morning held bottled water, beer, and more jugs for Barney. Jimmy jumped up and down, waving his arms and yelling something I couldn't hear.

"We did it, man," I told Barney, grinning, exhausted, my leg on fire. "We beat that rat. Now she'll have no choice but to have dinner with us. Er, with me."

Dropping my reins on Barney's neck, I lifted both my arms, making a V for victory sign with my hands. As I drew closer to the vehicles, I saw a movement in the shade near the two-horse trailer.

A gray horse turned on its lead rope to look at us. No saddle sat on its back, and its bridle was gone. My jaw dropped.

Reba, a beer in her hand, stepped from around the trailer's rear to caress the rat that had beaten my boy. Slumping in the saddle, I rode up to her, observing her smirk.

"I don't suppose you saved me one of those?"

Chapter Five

Reba

I handed Dirk a beer without looking at him directly. Sweaty, dirty, and a dark stubble covering his jaws, he had to be the sexiest man I'd ever seen. If I glanced into his face, that glance could easily become a drooling stare. He'd been cute in school, a fellow every girl had a crush on. In his maturity, Dirk's cute had morphed into the kind of rakish appearance that any publisher might want pictured on the cover of a romance novel.

"Thanks." He popped the tab and all but drained the can in a single gulp. "Hot today."

"Yeah."

Jimmy unsaddled the exhausted and lathered buckskin, then Marsha started walking him out. "Is he gonna be all right?"

Dirk glanced at his horse. "Yeah, I'll baby him for a while, only light exercise." He turned to face me. "So what do you want as your prize?"

I noticed both Marsha and Jimmy had occupied themselves well away from Dirk and me, so obvious in their intentions of leaving us together I almost rolled my eyes.

"Nothing. Proving you wrong about my horse is enough."

"You sure did that, right enough."

Dirk ambled toward Khan, and, my suspicion and dislike of him uppermost in my mind, I followed. Deep down I knew he'd never harm Khan out of spite, but I still didn't want him near my best boy without me there to supervise. He walked around Khan, studying his legs and running his hand down his neck and shoulder.

"He's got great conformation," Dirk commented. "Now I see why you might want to keep him a stud."

"Unfortunately, my dad wouldn't permit it." I sighed, stroking Khan's soft face. "We already have a breeding stallion. He didn't want two."

Dirk draped his arm over Khan's neck in what I could almost call affection, his eyes meeting mine. He smiled slightly. "I suppose I should quit calling him a rat."

"Makes no never mind to me," I replied. "I know his value."

"Come to dinner with me."

"You lost."

"So? I still want to take you to dinner."

I hesitated, sensing his masculine charisma stealing my willpower. I disliked him intensely, yet he possessed a magnetism, a mature sincerity that defined him now as a man. No longer the arrogant football player and rodeo king I once knew, he was now Dirk the soldier who'd saved lives, and he looked at me with hope.

"Why?"

"I could say I owe you for not just helping me but to make up for treating you the way I did. Dinner isn't even the start of paying back what I owe."

"You can just forget about it."

"Can you?"

Strangely, I couldn't look at him. I stared at Khan instead, my emotions churning into a wild mess I couldn't untangle.

"No."

"Neither can I. I'd like to get to know you."

"We've known each other all our lives, jeez."

"We've both grown up," he said quietly. "Matured. You're different now, though you don't believe me when I say I am, too. I'd like to show you what I've become."

"I don't like you very much, Blackburn."

He grinned, chuckling. "I'd like to change that."

So why was I so very tempted to accept his invitation? I absently watched Jimmy and Marsha as they examined Dirk's gelding, running their hands down his legs. Unable to sort out my mixed feelings, I finally nodded.

"Okay."

"Great." His genuine pleasure showed clearly on his face, in his brilliant blue eyes.

"What will your father say?" I asked.

"Same as yours, I expect," he replied. "Get mad, then get over it."

I thought of my father stabbing his finger at me, his dark, fierce expression behind it when he ordered me to stay away from Dirk. *He can't tell me what to do.*

"When and where?"

***

I'd dated a few guys since high school, even once went on a blind date Marsha set up. Not even the blind date made me as nervous as going out to dinner with Dirk. No, it wasn't what my parents would say if they found out. I didn't even tell them I had a date, much less who with.

My nervousness stemmed from going to dinner with the same person whom I'd feared and hated for so very long. What will we talk about? Could this be an elaborate trick designed to set me up? Make me think he's truly interested in being friendly only to smash me into pieces? Raising my defenses, I drove into the restaurant's parking lot and spotted Dirk's fancy Ram.

I wore a nice lavender blouse tucked into my jeans with a silver chain as a belt. With my hair loose rather than in its usual braid, I crossed the lot to the entrance, expecting Dirk to already be at a table. Instead, he sat just inside the door, waiting.

"You look great," he said, smiling as he stood. Like I did, he wore a button-down shirt, jeans, and boots, his black hair brushed neatly. Without his hat, his brilliant eyes contrasted sharply against his tanned flesh.

"You're incredibly beautiful."

My defenses weren't ready for that. Not one bit. I knew I blushed. I couldn't stop the heat from climbing into my cheeks.

"Uh, thanks. Been waiting long?"

"Nope. Our table is ready, I'm told."

The hostess who led us to our table couldn't keep her eyes from Dirk. Nor could I blame her. I struggled to not stare and drool over his hunky and ruggedly handsome face, the muscles that bulged under his shirt, the way he moved with a sinuous grace. Dirk touched my back lightly as we walked, electrifying me with a shiver of pleasure.

"Your waiter will be with you shortly." After another long look at Dirk, she left menus on the table and left.

"You must get that all the time," I commented.

"Get what?" Dirk seemed genuinely confused as he frowned.

"You didn't see her undressing you with her eyes?" I laughed.

"Oh. That." Dirk shrugged. "Yeah, but I tend to ignore it. Not worth troubling over. Don't you get that shit from guys?"

"No. If they stare at me, I never notice it."

Dirk leaned forward, his eyes intent. "You need to pay attention to what's going on around you, Reba. A gal with your looks can attract the wrong sort."

"Like you?" I smiled.

"Not my sort. The bad ones. The ones that might physically do you harm."

"All women are subjected to that behavior, Dirk," I said quietly. "Not just the pretty ones."

"My emphasis is on knowing who and what are around you," he went on. "Be prepared for anything."

"That sounds like the soldier talking."

He smiled. "It's not like I can take it off and hang it in the closet."

The waitress arrived to take our drink orders. Dirk lifted his brow while glancing at me.

"Wine?"

"Sure."

"What do you like?"

"A blush," I answered. "The house wine is good."

"Two, then."

She left us alone, staring at one another. I felt my defenses trickle away as Dirk's charismatic persona worked wonders on my slowly building trust.

"What did you do in the army?" I asked.

"Learned to fight. Then fought." He smiled. "Becoming disciplined and shooting at people who are trying to shoot you and your buddies, even killing the enemy… well, it tends to put things in perspective."

"I heard you're a decorated hero," I commented, "saved some lives."

Dirk glanced away from me, his eyes distant, his expression neutral.

"I took out the enemy fighters who had my patrol pinned down. Several of my unit were injured. I charged the nest, tossed in a grenade, shot those that survived the blast." He looked back at me. "It wasn't heroic. It was war, and what I had to do to keep my unit from getting their heads blown off."

"It sounds like a true act of courage, Dirk," I murmured. "Exposing yourself to enemy fire."

"I got lucky." He smiled sadly. "There are some that weren't."

The naked vulnerability I found in his eyes, his expression, tore at my heart. I once considered Dirk the most vile and despicable human on earth. Now I wanted to reach across the table and take his hand. To hold him close to me, to offer solace, to pull his pain from him.

My defenses weren't down far enough, however.

"I'm sorry," was all I could think of to say.

"War and killing isn't fun for anyone," he commented lightly. "Unfortunately, it's a way of life over there."

The waitress returned with our wine and pulled her order pad from her pocket. "Are you ready to order?"

Dirk and I both hastily looked at the menus. As this restaurant specialized in steaks, I ordered a medium rare rib-eye with shrimp and a salad.

"Make that two," Dirk said, handing his menu to the waitress.

He lifted his glass of wine. "Here's to a new start."

"I can drink to that."

We clicked glasses, and in that moment, something clicked between us. I sipped my wine, unsure of just what had happened. Perhaps my intense dislike of him had morphed into friendship, or at least friendliness. Maybe my attraction to him had turned into the first feelings of falling in love. All I knew was that Dirk and I now had a very strong connection. One that I didn't want to see break.

***

"This is great," he said, wiping his mouth on his napkin. He picked up his wine glass. "A perfect dinner with the most beautiful girl in town."

Over the steaks and shrimp, we'd talked at ease, laughed together, the hurt and anger from our past falling away like melting snow.

"I think I'll be the envy of all the single gals around here."

"Does that mean you'll let me take you out again?" His blue eyes gleamed with humor and warmth. "Become a steady thing?"

I chuckled. "Maybe. If you don't resort to bullying."

"Oh, hell no," he replied with a laugh. "I was so stupid back then, so damn immature. You know the old saying, had I known then what I know now…"

"I suppose with experience comes wisdom."

"Exactly. I really have changed, Reba, and so have you. In spite of everything, you're willing to let the past stay there."

"I guess I put things into perspective, too," I said quietly, liking the way he looked at me with appreciation and candor. The way a guy looked at a girl he really liked. "We were kids, and kids can be cruel without realizing the consequences of it."

"I'm really glad you hauled my ass out of that ravine."

"Fate?" I smiled, mischievous.

"Why not? I can't think of a better reason we're here now, enjoying one another's company."

"And that everything happens for a reason?" I nodded thoughtfully. "Could be. But at least we're not enemies anymore, even if our families are."

"Yeah, that sucks," he said. "If we're going to see each other, we'll have to stay under the radar."

"Oh, that'll be fun." I considered the possibility of simply being candid with my parents and telling them I'd see Dirk if I wanted to. *And I'll be disowned, excommunicated if not killed outright.* "My dad will pitch a fit."

"So will mine."

"Maybe over time we can make them see reason," Dirk added after a lengthy pause. "Get them to agree to disagree and let the family feud die away."

"My dad won't—"

His cell rang from his pocket, interrupting what I'd planned to say.

"Sorry," Dirk muttered, pulling his phone out to look at the screen. "Shit, it's my dad."

"Uh, oh."

Dirk clicked to answer it. "Hey, Dad."

I heard Billy Blackburn's voice through the speaker but couldn't understand his words. Dirk's mouth tightened in either worry or anger, his eyes on me.

"Okay, yeah," he said. "Right. I'm on my way."

"What's wrong?" I asked as he clicked off.

"I'm so sorry," he replied, standing while pulling out his wallet. "I have to go. Our barn caught fire."

Chapter Six

Dirk

Red and blue flashing lights pierced the late-night darkness. In the broad, graveled yard between the ranch houses and the barns, I saw at least three fire engines, two sheriff's department squad cars, and an ambulance. I parked my truck near my house, and the sight of the ambulance sent my pulse to pounding. *Did something happen after Dad called me?*

I sucked in the acrid stench of smoke and ash, tasting it on my tongue as I trotted past the firetrucks and firemen in their heavy fireproof coats and helmets. None tried to stop me as I headed for my parents, who were huddled together talking with animated gestures to the county sheriff.

"Dad, Mom," I gasped, encircling them both in a group hug. "Are you okay?"

"Yeah, we're fine," Mom said, shaking in my arms. "Tito was passing the barn and saw the flames."

"He yelled for us," Dad continued for her, his expression tight in the flashing lights. "He grabbed a fire extinguisher and started fighting it while we got the horses out."

"Were any hurt?" I released them and shook Sheriff Brody's hand.

"Hi, how are you?"

"Good, you?" Sheriff Brody had been the county sheriff when I was a kid, and now he owned a full head of silver hair.

"Nice to see you again, Dirk."

"Not very pleasant circumstances, though."

I gazed past him to the big barn, observing the firemen striding in and out, only a faint tendril of smoke curling up to vanish into the night.

"How bad?"

"Tito was on it like a tick on a coon," Brody drawled. "Wasn't anywhere near where you stored hay, thank God, but burned through the roof. A couple of stalls, too."

"None of the horses were burned?" I demanded, shooting a look at my father, Billy.

"Tito's checking them over," Billy answered. "It don't look like it. The stalls he's talking about were in the back corner. Didn't have any horses in them."

I blinked, thinking back.

"But I put your colts in those corner stalls yesterday."

Billy breathed deeply, visibly relaxing. "And Tito turned them out to let them stretch their legs. They're in the arena along with all the others."

"How lucky is that?" I asked with a chuckle. "We caught a break on that, didn't we?"

"Sure did," Billy agreed. "None of yours were hurt, Dirk. We just opened stalls and ran them out. We'd just got them all caught and in the arena when you got here."

"And Cutter?" I asked, thinking of how unsociable our breeding stallion was. *If he's in the arena, too, we'll have some hurt animals.*

"I shoved him in a stall over yonder." Billy waved a hand at the smaller barn where we mostly kept equipment and hay. "He's kicking up a racket what with all this going on."

"If you're okay, I'm going to find Tito," I said, my hand on my mom's shoulder.

"Yeah, yeah, go," Dad replied, impatient.

Leaving my folks with Brody, I walked quickly into the darkness beyond the emergency strobes and the lights from the houses. Apparently, the fire cut the barn's power, or it was cut off because of the fire. Either way, I passed its black maw and rounded the corner. I followed Tito's voice as he talked to the horses milling in the big arena.

"Hey, you big dummy, this ain't no big deal. Quit chasing Barney around. Barney, you kick her head off, you ain't no chickenshit."

I listened to hooves thudding the ground and caught sight of tossing heads and manes as the group that normally didn't mix with one another sorted out the pecking order. I reached Tito just as two horses galloped past, the one in the rear with teeth bared while the lead horse kicked backward in self-defense.

"Are they okay?"

"Yeah." Tito snorted. "Just letting them quiet down. That old boss mare is getting everybody all riled up."

"We might have to catch her," I suggested, "and stick her in the small barn with Cutter."

"Yep. Ain't gonna catch her until she settles, no way."

"Shit." In the darkness, with hooves and twelve-hundred-pound bodies running in all directions, Tito and I could easily be kicked or run over. "In a few, we'll throw some hay out. The mare will come eat, and we can catch her then."

"Yep."

I looked at his rugged profile in the near darkness. "None were burned?"

"Not that I can tell," Tito answered. "They was all run out real quick-like. Took all three of us to catch 'em, get 'em in here."

"Makes me glad they're easy to catch."

Tito chuckled. "Damn right. Get a bucket of grain, they all think they'll starve to death if they don't get to that bucket."

"What started the fire, Tito?"

He shook his head. "Don't know, man. Electrical, I think, as it was over by the outlet. It shouldn't have shorted, though, right?"

"I wouldn't think so."

"I'm gonna get that old bitch some feed," Tito grumbled. "She ain't gonna let up teaching them youngsters she's big and bad."

He left my side and vanished, still muttering under his breath, as I leaned against the arena rails. Our barn's electrical system was the same age as the barn—ten years old. Modern and up to date, it shouldn't have shorted and caused a fire. But what else could it be? No employee smoked in the barn. And as we had a total of three employees, one of them Jimmy, I also knew none of them smoked at all.

Nor did I or my parents.

Arson? I eliminated that thought right away. We had no enemies except the Sewells, and I knew neither Reba nor her father would do such a thing. *Shit, I was with Reba all evening. That's a damn good alibi.* I pondered other possibilities that might cause a barn fire and felt grateful for Tito spotting it in time.

He returned with a few flakes of hay and a can of sweet feed.

"C'mere, you old knot head," he called, tossing the hay into the arena and shaking the can. "Come get it."

At the sound and scent of the tempting feed, the old broodmare, who'd birthed several fine horses for the ranch, trotted across the ground toward us. Tito poured the grain onto the hay. After driving off a few challengers to her prize, she started to eat. Tito slipped through the rails and put a halter on her.

"She's just upset over the noise and commotion," Tito commented, stroking her neck. "They all are."

"So am I," I agreed. "Shit, this could have been bad. Thanks for being here at the right time, man."

"Yeah, I'm glad, too."

"I'm headed back," I continued. "Want to see if the firemen know what started it. I'll be back in a few."

"It's all good."

Leaving him, I went back to the front of the barn. Now Mom and Dad were talking with two firemen as well as Brody. One fire truck had turned off its emergency strobes and driven away, as had the second sheriff's cruiser and the ambulance. Firemen worked to coil hoses, bantering back and forth with one another.

"That was arson," Billy snarled as I joined the group. "No way was it electrical."

Brody sighed down his nose. "Arson is unlikely, Billy. We don't need the county arson investigator here nosing around."

"From what I found," the fire chief, whose name I couldn't remember, added, "it was a short. Came from the outlet where the fire started."

"Our system was updated," Billy roared, furious. "That's impossible."

The chief and Brody eyed one another uncomfortably.

"Billy, you need to calm down," Brody said. "Listen to him. Shorts happen in even the most modern systems. Who would want to burn your barn, anyway?"

"Sewell," my father snapped. "Brian, I want you to arrest him. I know he did it. He's always hated us."

Brody sucked in a deep breath. "That old feud is dead, man. Get over it. Rupert Sewell is too frigging old to be creeping around late at night setting fires. Use your damn head."

Billy, to my alarm, invaded Brody's space to glare eye to eye.

"Then it was his kid," he growled. "That girl who works for him. She did it."

"Dad," I protested. "Reba didn't do this."

"Dirk, you never mind." Billy didn't look away from Brody. "You go over there, Brian, and you investigate this as *arson*. I want them *behind* bars by *noon* tomorrow."

"This isn't the wild west," Brody snapped. "There are laws and procedures. I need proof, and right now I got jack shit."

Brody held my father's gaze. Seeing he wasn't about to back down, the chief released a sigh of surrender.

"The arson investigator is very good," the chief said mildly. "He'll know what caused it. I'll get him here as soon as I can."

"That's not good enough," Billy yelled. "That insane clan tried to burn down my barn, kill my horses. Just like Sewell's great-granddad did."

"Dad," I groaned. "Put that grievance down, it's more than a hundred years old now. Christ, this wasn't arson."

"What do you know?" he retorted. "How do you know? You were out with some broad getting laid or something."

"William!"

My mom, Samantha, a somewhat Puritan lady who never cussed, glared at Billy.

"Don't talk like that, that's rude. Dirk can go out with whomever he wants. He's an adult, if you hadn't noticed."

"Yeah, yeah," Billy griped, still glaring at the chief. "I want that arson investigator here, dammit. And when he proves Sewell did this, I want an apology from you both. Got it?"

"Billy, you need to just calm *down*," Brody said, his voice hard. "You're upset, I get it, but you can't just throw out accusations and hope one sticks. If Sewell didn't do this, and you accuse him anyhow, you can get sued, you know. If the chief says it was an accident, then it was a fucking *accident*." He eyed my mother. "'Scuse my French."

"If Sewell didn't do it, then his bitch of a daughter did," Billy insisted. "They're all no-good thieves and barn-burners. Nothing good comes from that blood."

Now my anger shot through the roof. "That's enough, Dad," I barked. "I told you Reba didn't do this. She didn't set this fire, and you know it. Shit, I told you, she hauled me from the damn ravine last month."

Billy's hot gaze, which had melted lesser men than me, turned to meet mine.

"And just *how* do you *know* she isn't a fire starter?"

I bit my tongue, trying to stop it, but I couldn't hold back.

"Dammit, she was with me tonight. I asked her out on a *date*, and she accepted. The best alibi you can ask for, Dad. She was with *me*."

As I spoke, Billy's expression turned cold, as hard as granite, and just as forgiving. My mother gasped in horror while I heard Brody mutter, "Oh, shit."

"You what?" Billy's voice had softened. Dangerously soft.

I hadn't faced enemy rifles or killed men by quavering in front of my pissed-off father.

"I asked her out," I snapped, leaning toward him. "I *like* her. She's kind, sweet, beautiful, and I plan to ask her out again. Like it or not, Dad—I *will* see Reba again."

"Like hell you will," he growled. "You can date anyone in the world. *Except* Reba Sewell. Do you understand me?"

"Billy—"

"You don't tell me who I can and can't see," I rumbled, furious. "You're living in the past, harboring grudges more than a hundred years old. I've *faced* grudges like that in Afghanistan, killed men who've held religious grievances for centuries, and you *don't* tell me what to do."

"Don't I?" Billy's lips thinned to the point they vanished. "You're no son of mine. You don't live on this ranch anymore. Get out of my sight."

Chapter Seven

Reba

"His dad kicked him out."

I gaped at the kitchen's far wall, my glass of juice raised halfway to my mouth.

"No way."

"Yes, way. Dirk is staying with Jimmy in town," Marsha said, her tone low. "Jimmy said there was a fire at the Sewell place last night."

"Yeah, I know," I said, setting my glass down. "Dirk told me."

"Jimmy said Dirk took you out last night."

"Yeah. He did."

Marsha's squeal nearly burst my eardrum. "Oh, my God, that is so cool! I can see you two together, I really can."

"Knock it off," I ordered. "So why did Blackburn kick Dirk out?"

"According to Jimmy, Billy Blackburn was accusing *you*, my dear, of arson."

"What? Me?"

"Well, Dirk said you couldn't have done it. He took you to dinner after all. Perfect alibi."

I groaned and closed my eyes. "So *that's* why Blackburn kicked him out."

"Yeah. Totally Romeo and Juliette here, baby. No suicide, okay? Promise?"

"Shut up." I nibbled my lip, thinking. "What will Dirk do now?"

"I don't know. Jimmy says he won't show up for work, so old Blackburn is stuck without two cowhands. Will that make that old fart take Dirk back?"

"I have no idea. All the Blackburns are nuts."

Marsha laughed. "So sure, are you?"

"Okay, maybe Dirk is all right."

"He's more than all right, admit it. Have a good time?"

I smiled. "Yeah. He's really cool, very sweet. Admitted that what he did in school was stupid, just being kids."

"I told you, Jimmy said he's changed. You like him?"

Her sly tone had me laughing. "Let's say I'm letting the past go."

"Will you see him again?"

I hesitated. Marsha read me correctly and laughed.

"Yeah, you will. Reba, he's a gem, a keeper. Give him a chance, okay? Promise?"

"I'll give him a chance."

***

After I fed and watered the horses, the chickens, the few cows and calves we kept in a corral, I mucked stalls and dumped the manure in the compost pile. As I worked, I knew I needed to see

Dirk. Marsha told me where Jimmy lived in town, and I didn't tell my folks where I was headed before I jumped into my truck.

I recognized Dirk's Ram parked beside Jimmy's beat-up Chevy in the driveway as I parked in front of the house. Feeling guilty for a crime I didn't commit, I walked to the front door and rang the bell. Only a screen door prevented a visitor from entering the bungalow. A vicious, loud barking answered the doorbell, and I stepped back in terror as a big, fast, gray and brown dog rushed toward me, its teeth gleaming pure white.

Oh, shit, it's gonna come right through the screen. I'm so dead.

Dirk's voice cracked over the dog's snarling. I didn't understand what he ordered, but the dog obeyed. And obeyed instantly. It turned to lope back the way it came as Dirk, a beer in his hand even at this early hour, came to the door. He grinned.

"Hi."

"Uh, hi." I tried looking past him to where the mutt might be lurking, ready to chew my throat out. "I heard you were here."

He swung the door open. "C'mon in."

"Am I, er, gonna survive if I do?"

He chuckled. "That's Magnum. He's my dog from the war, saved my life. Once he knows you, he's a mush. Come on, he's okay."

Still worried, I stepped cautiously into the house. The dog lay panting in the far room, watching me, but not with any aggression that I recognized. Dirk spoke a few words in a language I didn't know, and the dog trotted toward us. He sniffed me over, his tail high and wagging, then licked my hand.

"What language is that?" I asked, rubbing the dog's head and ears as he waggled around my legs like a puppy.

"Czech," Dirk answered. "I taught him all his commands in that language so no one could use him against me. Yeah, he's trained to kill, and he has. Want a beer?"

"It's not even noon."

Dirk shrugged. "I'll take that as a yes."

I followed him into the kitchen. The dog, a Belgian Malinois, if I knew my breeds, bounded behind with his tail high. I saw no sign of Jimmy and sat at the worn kitchen table as Dirk opened the fridge.

"Marsha said your dad thinks I started that fire."

"He does." Dirk set a beer in front of me, then took a chair opposite. "Don't sweat it. We both know where you were."

Magnum shoved his head under my arms for affection. As I caressed his silky coat, I met Dirk's grim gaze.

"Look, I have to say I'm sorry this happened."

"Me, too."

He took a swallow of his beer. "It sucks, but what can I do?" He smiled, and that smile lit his face into something that wasn't cute, wasn't handsome, but beautiful.

"What will you do?"

"I dunno. Get a job on another ranch, find a place." His smile deepened. "Ask you out, make you fall in love with me."

"Oh, you think that'll happen?" I smirked. A tingle started somewhere in my stomach and spread. "You're cocky."

"I know what I want."

"And you want me?"

He set his beer down and leaned forward. "I want to see where you and I can go. Is that okay?"

I realized that it was very much okay. I, too, wanted to see where this could go. "It's cool."

"Great." He sat back and drank from his can. "My dog likes you."

I lowered my face so Magnum could give me a wet, sloppy kiss. "And that's a recommendation?"

"You know it. If my dog doesn't like a person, that person doesn't live long."

"No way."

"Look, he's been trained to protect me. We've both been in combat. His instincts for people are dead on, they have to be. He knows an enemy when he confronts one."

I stared down into happy brown eyes that stared up into mine, Magnum's jaws wide in a happy grin. "I can hardly believe this is the dog you're describing, Dirk. He's like a friendly puppy."

"To the good ones." Dirk smirked. "Congrats. You're one of the good ones."

I cupped Magnum's jowls. "You're just a big softie, aren't you?"

Dirk snorted. "Don't get him started."

Magnum, all seventy-five pounds of him, literally crawled into my lap. Slightly worried about my exposed throat so close to fangs that have killed, I needn't have been. The mutt busily licked my cheek, my ear, his tail wagging happily.

"What a sweet dog."

"Does your old man know about us?" Dirk asked somewhere behind the heavy pile of muscle and fur filling my arms.

"No. I'd thought to be upfront about seeing you, but after what yours did, I'm not so sure that's a good idea."

"Probably not. He might kick you out."

I urged Magnum onto the floor but continued to rub his neck and ears. "Yeah, he already forbade me to see you."

"After you told him you helped me?"

I nodded. "At the time, it was easy to say I wasn't going to. Will your dad change his mind and ask you to come home?"

"No idea. And I'm not sure I will if he does."

I looked down at Magnum, once again feeling guilty for something that wasn't my fault. "This just sucks," I muttered.

"Yeah." Dirk leaned forward over the table. "It's up to you and me to end this damn feud. Let them hate one another all they want, we'll decide what *we* want. When we see where this goes."

I pondered the implications of this. To date Dirk, to perhaps fall in love and become estranged from my parents, just as Dirk now was? Is that what I wanted? To make a choice between my folks and Dirk? I didn't like that. Rupert could be a hard case when it came to Dirk's family, but I loved him. And my mother.

"One step at a time, okay?" I asked softly. "Maybe we can convince our folks to simply blow this whole feud off."

"Maybe."

***

Hiding around the corner of the barn, I watched my parents climb into their pickup and head for town, a plume of dust kicked up by the tires hovering in the nearly still air. In the month since I'd started secretly dating Dirk, the summer had grown hot without the usual rain. The cattle on the various ranches at the feet of the Bitterroot range grazed on brown, not green, grass.

Once they'd driven out of sight, I led Khan and a rangy bay gelding from the barn. Since I'd already saddled and bridled them, I mounted Khan and led the bay by his bridle from the barnyard. As Dirk's horse, the buckskin named Barney, was still stuck at his dad's ranch, I always brought one of ours for him to ride on our riding dates.

And we'd had many of these since we'd called our private truce.

Dirk waited by his parked truck a half mile down the dirt road from our driveway. Magnum, busy chasing the deflated football Dirk threw for him, galloped madly down the road to meet me. Still clutching the football, he danced under Khan's hooves, growling.

"Hi."

I bent from my saddle to kiss Dirk, a sensuous and erotic kiss that held the promise of more to come. He scented of cologne and of masculine alpha male, smiling up at me with his hand on my thigh. Taking the bay's reins, he vaulted into the saddle, then found his stirrups.

"I thought we might head over to the creek," he commented. "Let the horses get a drink while we hang out."

"Sounds good to me."

Hand in hand, our knees bumping as we rode, we talked about horses, cattle, and our work, keeping the conversation well away from our parents. Despite the arson investigator informing Billy Blackburn that the barn fire was indeed accidental in nature, he refused to acknowledge Dirk or invite him to return home.

"I'm thinking of making an offer on the Hopper Ranch," Dirk said as we tied our horses in the shade near the burbling creek. "The old man is dying, and his kids don't want it."

Panting heavily in the heat after his long run at our horses' feet, Magnum drank from the creek, then plopped in the shade to cool off.

"That's a nice place," I remarked. "Better grazing than lots of ranches around here."

"Yeah. His asking price is rock bottom, too."

Dirk seized me around my waist before I could sit on a large rock next to the creek. My arms crept around his neck as his tongue slid into my mouth. An erotic tingle started somewhere around my navel and worked downward, my pussy quivering with anticipation. His hard chest pressed against my breasts as he pulled me fully against him, letting me feel the iron bulge beneath his belt buckle.

He broke our kiss, but his lips nibbled mine. "Okay?"

"Okay."

Pulling me down with him onto a sandy patch of ground free from rocks, Dirk lifted my tank top over my head. He helped me slide my jeans down, then my panties. My aching tunnel dripped my arousal as I lay back, the sand hot under my skin. I drank in his impossibly broad shoulders, tapering down to trim hips, his chest and arms bulging with muscle as he quickly undressed.

I caught my breath at the sight of his impressive erect shaft hanging stiffly from his thatch of black pubic hair.

"Wow."

Dirk knelt beside me. "I swear I'll be gentle."

I stroked my fingers up and down its velvety soft length, its iron hardness, then down to cup his balls.

"It's beautiful," I murmured.

"You're beautiful."

He lay down beside me, his fingers dipping deep into my pussy even as he French kissed me again. Growing as hot as the sand under me, I nearly came as he teased me into a near orgasm. His talented tongue sent me over the edge in sheer erotic pleasure.

Barely able to close my fist around his cock, I passed my hand up and down its length, making him groan deep in his throat.

Leaving my mouth, Dirk licked and sucked on my hard nipples, the exquisite sensations driving me crazy with lust and need. I wanted him badly, wanted him on me, in me, filling me to the brim with that monster organ. I tried to pull him onto me, but he resisted, continuing to tease me until I thought I'd go mad.

"I need you," I gasped. "C'mon."

Dirk rolled atop me, kissing my cheeks, my throat, my eyes, his knees spreading my legs wide. I gasped at the first touch of his cockhead at the entrance of my pussy, feeling him spear me, spread me wide. As he promised, he worked his way in slowly, one shallow thrust at a time. The pleasure of his cock in me boiled over.

I cried out as I orgasmed, my pussy throbbing, quivering under my intense climax. I clutched Dirk hard to me and my legs clamped over his as he drove in further and further still. His strong hands under my ass lifted me, creating a steeper angle that permitted him to thrust harder, faster.

"You're mine," he muttered thickly in my ear. "You're mine always, forever."

Chapter Eight

Dirk

Our oily sweat mingled under the bright sunlight and the intense pleasure of our lovemaking. Reba's perfect body, her tight muscles and firm belly, forced me to control my explosion just from looking at her. Without a doubt in my mind, I'd fallen hard in love with her, and our mutual pleasuring of one another cemented it in my heart.

I loved her.

And the worry that she didn't feel the same niggled in the back of my mind.

I stroked in and out, panting, gasping, my brow on the sand beside her face, her nails digging into my back in her extreme second orgasm. She shivered and quaked under me, her body stiffening, her pussy undulating, squeezing my cock. I couldn't hold back any longer. I came, moaning, becoming as stiff as Reba, my thrusts slowing but plunging in deeper than ever. My orgasm rolled me under, and I felt as though it would continue for hours and kill me as a result.

It did end, however. I breathed hard and let Reba's legs slide down, my semi-hard cock still buried inside her. Nor did she seem eager to have me off, despite the heat and our sweat. Half-thinking of a wash in the icy creek, I raised myself up enough to gaze into her beautiful face.

"Okay?"

Reba sighed and half-laughed. "More than okay. You're a very generous lover. I never have two orgasms in a row."

I kissed her tenderly, sweetly, propping myself up on my elbow in order to swipe a tendril of hair from her face.

"Reba." I hesitated, then blurted it out. "I love you."

For a moment, shock and fear filled her eyes, and in that instant, I knew my hopes were in vain. *She'll say that's nice, but I can't love you in return.* Then she smiled, her hands on the back of my neck.

"I really tried not to," she murmured. "I reminded myself time and again how much I hated you."

Confused, I rolled off of her delectable body and sat bare-assed on the sand. Magnum ambled over, still panting, and licked salty sweat from my shoulder.

"What do you mean?"

"I wish I could say I don't love you." Reba also sat up, hugging her knees to her breasts as though cold. "I do. I fell hard for you, Dirk."

"You—you did?" Then I broke out laughing and bent to kiss her. "You love me. And I love you. That's great."

Her smile faded. "So what do we do about our folks? Your dad disowned you. Mine might disown me. But I can't hide it from them anymore. It's too damn hard to sneak around, you know? As a kid, it seemed easy. Now?" She sighed. "It's a pain in the ass."

I stood up and held my hand down to her. "We'll think of something. Meanwhile, how about a wash in the water?"

"Oh, man, yeah." Reba accepted my help and also stood. "I'm covered in sand."

The icy water rushed over my cringing feet as I stepped into the creek. Reba squealed as she bent to toss water over her naked and perfect body. Laughing, excited as little kids, we splashed each other while Magnum, barking, plunged back and forth between us. Despite the heat, I shivered when I stepped from the water, and my cock shriveled to the size of an anemic peanut.

"I got sand up my works," Reba commented, sitting in the water to finish washing.

Magnum jumped around her, licking her face and mock growling in an effort to get her to play with him. She eyed me after pushing him away.

"You sure this is the same dog you had over there? This isn't a war dog, he's a fool."

I dressed as she finally stepped, sleek and running with wet, from the creek. I couldn't take my eyes from her.

"He's the same dog. Come Fourth of July, both of our PTSDs will come out. I don't know what I can do to protect him from the noise."

Reba flipped her wet hair over her shoulders, then tugged on her panties, then her jeans.

"Both of you should go away, go for a drive up in the high mountains and stay there for a few days."

I paced over to her and kissed her. "Will you come with us?"

I sure loved her slow smile, the delight in her eyes when she looked at me.

"Why not?"

***

His claws sliding over the truck's leather seat, Magnum fought against falling to the floor as I bounced the Ram over the deep ruts of the ranch road. Reba, riding shotgun, gazed out her window at the Bitterroot Mountains. There, the pines gave way to grazing Hereford cattle on the wide prairie grassland.

"Jimmy might join with us in a partnership," I said, hitting yet another deep rut. "What do you think?"

"I think it's a good idea," Reba replied. "This ranch is huge, and running it will take more than the two of us."

Grinning, I took her hand over the console. "I like the sound of that."

"It's a practical standpoint," she went on after a laugh. "With Jimmy's experience with horses, we can breed and train top stock to sell. Isn't Mr. Hopper including the stock in the deal?"

"Yeah," I replied, braking at the top of a hill. "Let's take a look."

We stepped out, and I opened the rear door for Magnum. I took Reba's hand as we gazed out over the valley below, at the cattle, at the stream that ran through the property, at the magnificent view of the jagged mountain peaks.

"He said he'd rather not sell his horses and cattle before selling the property," I said, my arm over her shoulders. "Since he knows me, us, he knows we won't abuse his stock."

"And doesn't he have a former halter futurity champion that later won the World Championships in reining?" Reba asked. "Is he included in the sale?"

"I think so, yeah. A big-name stud, but he's getting old now. Might be in his twenties."

Reba shrugged. "You testosterone-laden males can reproduce even in your old age. I bet he has a few more good breeding years in him."

"So what are you thinking?"

"Mr. Hopper hasn't really promoted him lately," she replied. "We start promoting, get decent mares in the first year at a reasonable stud fee, then gradually increase it. We also breed him to good mares, train and sell his progeny. With Jimmy on board, we can train and sell reining winners."

I nodded slowly, gazing out over the land I hoped to own soon—with Reba and Jimmy.

"His offspring have done well at reining shows, I believe. With his cattle, we can take off right away. It might be hard the first year or so with the hefty mortgage. But we can make a go of it, right?"

"We can." Reba smiled up at me. "If we work hard, don't have a bad winter or three that kill off the cattle, we'll do fine."

I hugged her tight. "Think of it," I said, excited, pointing out over the green valley that spread for miles. "This will be ours. Ours!"

"Okay, ace." Reba pulled away from me to look into my eyes. "We'll be sharing that house with Jimmy? Now don't get me wrong, I like him, he'll be a good roommate. But what about later? If we have kids, he falls in love, gets married, has kids. See what I mean? That house is big, but it isn't *that* big."

"I got you covered, m'lady." I held her around her waist, smiling into her incredible eyes. "We'll build another house. There's plenty of room down there for a second house. Jimmy has already started making plans for it, where it'll sit, how many rooms, yada, yada."

Reba chuckled. "You boys have it all figured out."

"Yep. Now all we need to do is sell this to a loan officer."

She slid her arms around my waist, resting her face on my chest.

"That'll mean leaving my parents, Dirk. They rely on me to run the ranch."

"I know," I replied, my chin on the top of her head. "You're torn between me and your folks. I dig it."

"What do I do?"

"You'll do what's best for everyone, baby. Knowing you, you'll keep working for your dad while helping us with ours. Right?"

"I guess so."

"Look, the Hopper place runs adjacent to your ranch. So they're close. We'll make gates you can ride through, make it easier to handle both places."

Reba smiled up at me. "You're too smart to be a damn rancher."

I rubbed her shoulders. "Come on. Let's go have a chat with Hopper. See what he might have to say about our plans for his land."

***

"Jimmy!" I yelled, catching his attention as Reba and I, hand in hand, walked down the main street's sidewalk. "Get over here, you old shit. We have great news."

Jimmy, dodging traffic, trotted across the four-lane main drag that ran through our small town and joined us. He instantly hugged Reba, laughing, then thumped me on my shoulder.

"What's up, dude?" he asked, making sheep's eyes at Reba. "You two engaged now?"

"Er, not yet." I laughed. "Soon, though. Look, we had a talk with Mr. Hopper. Guess what?"

"Dude, I hate guessing games. Speak, or shut the fuck up."

"Mr. Hopper has dropped his price," Reba told him, grinning. "By almost *half*."

Disbelieving, Jimmy gaped, looking at me, then Reba, then back again. "Uh."

"He's mad at his kids for not following in his footsteps and for being greedy about the money they'll inherit. He's *pissed*." Laughing, I embraced Jimmy. "He doesn't want them inheriting what they *think* they will, and what he's asking for will see him through until he dies."

"And because it's *us* buying his property," Reba added, as excited as I was, "he wants to see us make a go of it."

"But," Jimmy stammered, his eyes flicking back and forth. "That price will make it easier for us to secure a loan. Amirite?"

I threw my arms around him. "Yeah, man. We're in the clear. We can *do* this."

Grabbing Reba, I danced with them in a three-way hug, laughing, yelling in delirious excitement. I would go into business with my best gal and my best friend, marry my best girl, make a good living here in Montana at the foot of the Bitterroot Mountains. Our future was not just secure, it was in the fucking *bag*.

"Reba?"

I'd never heard his voice before, but Reba halted her wild laughter and wilder dancing the instant it struck us. She stared past my shoulder, her mouth open, her face pale in shock, in fear, in consternation.

"Dad, Mom," she blurted. "Uh, hi."

I half turned, as did Jimmy. Rupert Sewell stood beside Brigitte, his wife, recent purchases in plastic bags dangling from their hands. Rupert flicked his glance between Reba, Jimmy, and me while Brigitte merely stared at Reba.

"What's going on?" Rupert asked, his gaze hardening as he recognized me. "What are you doing with Blackburn's kid?"

I had only a moment to admire her courage. Her hand in mine, Reba took two steps toward them.

"This is Dirk," she said, as though they had no idea who I was, "and—and I love him. He loves me. We're going to buy the Hopper Ranch. Together."

Chapter Nine

Reba

If I'd hoped for a softening of his expression, my hope died in vain. Dad's eyes narrowed in anger… no, *rage*, as he contemplated my hand in Dirk's.

"You're *what*?"

"I love him," I snapped, angry. "You forbade me to see him, but I did anyway. I'll still help you, and Mom, on the ranch. But we're buying our own place, with Jimmy."

My father, whom I'd once called loving, generous, and kind, paced forward, his blue eyes snapping in rage.

"No daughter of mine will consort with a *fucking* Blackburn."

Dirk, his hand still in mine, might have lunged at my dad. My firm grip held him back.

"You're as bad as my father," he growled, his blue eyes flat. "So wrapped up in this stupid feud, you can't see Reba's happiness. We love each other, moron. I *love* her. I'll take good care of her. She'll have a loving man, a future, maybe kids. *Your* grandchildren."

"No Blackburn bastard will fuck my daughter."

"Rupert!"

"Dad!" I yelled at the same time my mom whirled on my father. "I love Dirk, can't you see that? It's time to stop hating."

"I'll never stop hating the Blackburns."

"You motherfucker," Dirk yelled, lunging forward. Only my hand in his dragged him back, yet he almost yanked me off my feet. "You'll ruin Reba's happiness?"

"I don't care about her *happiness*," my father roared. "She'll get over you, you pig, and find a *decent* man to marry."

His hard words stunned me. I could only stare at him as his hot gaze met mine. I fumbled for something defiant, something as hurtful as his words to throw back into his teeth. But nothing came. Only the pain of what he'd said seeped into my heart. I turned my face away and buried it in Dirk's shoulder.

I no longer have a father.

"That's great," Dirk shouted, his arm over me, holding me under his strong arm. "You *bastard*. You'd murder Reba's soul for your own petty grievances? Go ahead, you shit. Tear her heart out, won't you?"

Jimmy's hand tapped us both.

"Uh, we have more trouble, kids. Billy and Sam are on the warpath, six o'clock."

I spun when Dirk did, facing his outraged parents coming from the opposite direction. *Oh, jeez, enough already! Why do we need to have a public quarrel in, um, public?*

"So you're still with that Sewell bitch," Billy Blackburn snapped, glaring at me. "Dump her now, and you can come home, Dirk."

"Just who are you calling a bitch?" Rupert snarled at the same time as Dirk's hot retort resounded. "Call her a bitch again and I'll punch your lights out."

"You know fucking well she isn't worth your spit," Billy grated, still glaring at me. "She's a damn Sewell."

"And a sight better than being a Blackburn," Rupert yelled, "Reba, get over here *now*. You're coming home with us."

"Dad—"

"Don't give me no lip, girl," Dad retorted. "I *said* now."

My rage and pent-up fury at this stupid and embarrassing fight on a city street rose, out of control.

"Knock it off, Dad," I shouted. "I love Dirk. Get with the program, will you? I'll come home when I'm ready to come home."

Rupert Junior stiffened, his gaze unforgiving, his face suffused with hot rage.

"Come with me now, Reba, or you'll never be welcome under my roof. Again."

"Rupert!" Mom yelled, slapping his shoulder. "That's *my* daughter you're condemning. My *daughter*."

"I don't care," I screamed. "If you can't accept the man I love, then the hell with you."

"Dirk, if you keep that bitch, I swear to God—"

Spinning without me, Dirk's fist rose. And he punched Billy hard across his jaw. Stumbling back, his eyes stunned, Billy raised his hand to his face and stared at Dirk. Swaying on his feet and bleeding from a split lip, he looked at his scarlet fingers, then at his son.

"I warned you," Dirk growled. "I warned you *not* to call her a bitch. Do it again, and you'll spend the night in the hospital."

A siren's scream split the hot air, cutting through the tension like a knife through butter. The sheriff's cruiser screeched to a halt at the curb, and Sheriff Brody lunged from behind the wheel.

"What the fuck is going on here?" he yelled, his hand on his gun. "Break up this bullshit before I haul all your asses off to jail."

I turned away, my heart stricken with sick fury, with guilt, with remorse, with the knowledge that whatever I decided, it would be the wrong decision. Go with Dirk, I alienate my parents. Leave Dirk, and I break my own heart. *This is so not fair!* I screamed inwardly. *I can't handle this. I have to get out of here.*

Leaving the small crowd to yell, to accuse, to shove one another, I slipped out from under Dirk's arm and fled. Running down the sidewalk, tears blinding me, all I could think of was escape. Escaping the madness, escaping the rage, and fleeing to the mountains. In the high country I might hide, heal, and one day come to grips with what or who I wanted out of life.

Ignoring my name being yelled from behind me, I ran home.

***

Mounted on Khan, I rode. My best friend, my equine soul mate, I rode him into the high elevations seeking peace and solitude. My cell rang unanswered in my back pocket. Dirk, my father, my mother, Jimmy, Marsha, they all called and left desperate messages. *Call me back. I'm worried about you.*

"Yeah? Well, tough shit."

Khan carried me along the high trails amid the boulders and the tall pines and evergreens, as loyal a companion as I'd ever needed or wanted. Solid, sure-footed, silent, he eased my spirit as no one ever could. With him, I could pour out my guts, my heart, my soul, and never be judged. Khan loved me, and I him. He didn't care about a century-old family feud. He cared about me.

Reining in at the top of the trail in a rocky clearing where the slope fell steeply downward, I hooked my knee around my saddle's horn and gazed out over the stunning vista. A bald eagle soared below us, its wings spread wide, then vanished around the mountain's flank. Drawing in a deep breath of the clean, high-altitude air, I tried to bring in peace and breathe out my emotional turmoil.

"What do I do?" I asked, watching Khan's ears flick backward. "I can't go home, but I have to take you back. What a clusterfuck."

Where will I go? I pondered my immediate future, half-thinking to call Marsha and ask if I could stay with her. Until I sorted out my feelings, my confusion, I needed to stay away from both Dirk and my parents. Still, I craved his arms around me, his kiss, his smile, his warm, loving eyes looking into mine.

It hit me then. Like a rock between my eyes, I made my choice. If my father can't accept that I'm deeply in love with Dirk, then so be it. If he can't let go of his silly hatred for the Blackburn name, then he'll be the one living with that choice. Not me. And not Dirk.

"C'mon," I said, swinging my leg back where it belonged, and picked up my stirrup. "We'd better head back. It'll be dark soon, and we don't need to have a run-in with a cougar."

I reined Khan around to follow the trail downhill, giving him his head and leaning back to help him find his balance. Agile and sure-footed, he crossed over the rocky and tree-choked terrain, startling the occasional deer. Having made my decision, I felt lighter, happier, now able to think of Jimmy, Dirk, and me buying the Hopper Ranch and working for ourselves and not our parents.

"Maybe one day they'll come to terms with this," I told Khan. "Though I hate to think of Dad hiring someone to replace me. That'll hit him where it hurts."

Upon reaching a low enough elevation where I could now make a call, I stood in my stirrups to wrangle my cell from my pocket. Darkness had set in, but this part of the trail was as familiar to me as my own backyard. Okay, so it *was* my backyard.

"Reba, where the hell have you been?" Marsha demanded. "I've been worried sick."

"I had to go for a ride," I told her, "get my head back where it should be."

"Your dad and Dirk's dad nearly got arrested, did you hear?"

"I think Brody was yelling that when I took off."

"Where are you?"

"Not far from my place," I replied, "but I'm only going to put Khan up, then leave."

"And go where? You can stay here, Jake won't mind."

"Thanks, I might take you up on it. But I want to talk to Dirk. I need to see him."

"Yes, do that. Jimmy called to ask if you had called and told me Dirk's out of his mind worrying about you."

"If it's okay with Jimmy, I might stay at his place with Dirk. This whole thing is a fucked-up mess."

"Damn. I know, baby," Marsha said, her tone low. "A flipping brawl in the middle of town." She chuckled. "I wish I'd seen it. But Jimmy went into graphic detail."

I rode Khan on a loose rein, my cell to my ear, not paying much attention to the dark woods around us.

"This Hatfields and McCoys bullshit needs to end," I groused. "How can Dirk and I have a decent future when our dads hate one another, Billy hates me, my dad hates Dirk? Jeez, can you see Christmas and Thanksgiving get-togethers?"

Marsha laughed. "Keep all the knives and guns locked up."

"They can do enough damage with their fists."

"Look on the bright side, girl," Marsha said cheerfully. "You got the most eligible bachelor in Montana."

"Yeah, I did, didn't I?"

Khan suddenly shied, dancing sideways, his head up. He stopped, staring into the darkness to our right, and snorted. That was his alarm signal that all wasn't right in his world. *A cougar?* A chill slid up my spine.

"Marsha, I gotta go. Something's wrong. There's something that Khan doesn't like."

"Oh, shit. Girl, you be careful. Get home as fast as possible."

"I'm not far from the barn. I'm worried it's a cougar."

Chapter Ten

Dirk

I heard her horse snort and Reba's low voice as she spoke to someone. My hand on Magnum's collar, I wondered how I might let her know what spooked her horse without sending him into a wild flight that might get Reba hurt. Arabs are such idiotic beasts.

I whistled a few notes. Listening intently, I heard the horse move forward again, his hooves crunching on twigs, his body brushing against the scrub oak.

"Dirk?"

"Yeah," I called softly. "I can't let your old man know I'm here. He might shoot to kill."

"We sure don't need that."

A shadow, darker than the night around us, appeared like a phantom. Magnum whined eagerly, his tail swinging his entire rear end back and forth. I let him go just as Reba dismounted. He crashed into her in delight and created enough noise to possibly alert Rupert in the house.

"Good dog," Reba told him as Magnum leaped up to wash her face, agreeing that he was indeed a good dog.

My intense relief at finding her safe and well nearly had me in tears. I held her tightly, breathing in her sweet scent, feeling her heartbeat against my chest.

"I love you. You had me so scared."

"I know," Reba murmured. "I'm sorry. I had to be alone for a while."

"I get it, I do. But don't ever do that again."

She chuckled and pulled away.

"How'd you know where I'd be?"

"I didn't. I just knew you took your horse, and that you'd come back here eventually."

"I don't want to go home," she said slowly. "Will Jimmy mind if I bunk with you?"

"He won't mind. My truck is parked on the road."

"Okay, I just have to put Khan up in the barn."

In the darkness so as not to alert her parents in the house, Reba untacked and curried her Arab while I put water and feed in his stall. Magnum trotted around the barn, sniffing the ground, then halted. His ears and muzzle pointed toward the large barn doors, and then he growled softly.

"To me," I ordered quietly in Czech.

Obeying instantly, he ran back to sit at my knee. I glanced at Reba, who'd also halted her task of currying the Arab. In frozen silence, we listened intently as footsteps trod outside the barn, paused at the doors, then paced on. When Magnum relaxed, I knew Rupert Sewell had ambled away.

"Let's go," I said, hurrying back to Reba. "Your dad might come back."

"I'm not in the mood for another confrontation."

"Me, either."

With Khan in his stall, I took Reba's hand and ordered Magnum to walk at heel. Creeping out into the dark night, I led the way past the outer sheds toward the forest that bordered the road. Keeping a wary eye out for Sewell, I tried my best to not make much noise while crunching over dead twigs. I finally breathed when we reached my truck.

"I don't think he'd actually shoot you," Reba commented, climbing into the cab.

"I'm not interested in taking the chance."

"Would your father try to shoot me?"

I shut the rear door behind Magnum.

"Again, let's not take any chances. They're both crazy."

***

Making sweet, tender love to Reba, then sleeping with her in my arms felt like a dream come true. She snored lightly, ladylike, as I propped my head on my arm to watch her sleep, bright sunlight streaming in through the sheer curtains. *I want this for the rest of my life, waking every morning to her lovely face beside me.*

Reluctant to leave the bed, I yawned, kissed her bare shoulder, then got up. Magnum stretched, yawning with his pink tongue hanging to his chest, then sat while I quietly dressed in my jeans and a t-shirt. Barefoot, I went down the stairs to let Magnum out the back door.

"You two kept me awake half the night," Jimmy grumbled, making coffee. "Have some decency, will you?"

"If you heard us," I replied around another yawn, "then you were listening at the door."

"Blow me."

"You're not my type."

Sitting at the table drinking coffee in companionable silence, I pondered the length of time it might take to acquire a loan, close on the Hopper Ranch, and move in. A month? Two? *The three of us can live here for a few months, piece of cake. We'll be living together for a long time.*

"I smell coffee."

Her blonde tresses tangled in an exotic mess over her shoulders and back. Reba padded barefoot to the pot and poured a cup.

"You two look like the aftereffects of a wild party."

"You and he had the party," Jimmy replied. "Now I need to get laid."

Magnum barked at the backdoor, a polite request to come in. I obliged him as Reba joined us at the table. He greeted her with doggy enthusiasm, then lay down on the floor with a grunt. Sipping her coffee, Reba glanced between Jimmy and me.

"So, what's on the agenda now?"

I shrugged. "Start shopping for a loan. A couple of us will have to find work."

"We all will," Reba began but was interrupted by the doorbell.

Instantly, Magnum raced down the hall barking like a mad thing. Standing and scowling at the early morning interruption, Jimmy followed him. I called Magnum back, and just as he sat beside my chair, I heard loud, angry voices.

"I know she's here," Rupert snapped, his heavy tread resounding in the hall.

"Hey, you can't just barge in here, man," Jimmy protested.

I grabbed Magnum's collar just as Rupert stormed into the kitchen. A low snarl started in Magnum's throat as he stared at the threat Rupert posed. Dismissing his menace as inconsequential, Rupert glowered at Reba.

"You're coming home with me," he snapped.

"Actually," she replied calmly, "I'm not. Do I have to call the cops, father mine?"

"Reba," he barked. "Let's go. And I'll forget all about you messing around with Blackburn."

"Get out," Jimmy yelled. "This is my house, and you can't just walk in here, dammit."

"I came for my daughter," Rupert retorted. "I'm not leaving without her."

"Care to bet on that?" I asked, catching his eyes. "You leave quietly, and I won't let go of this dog."

Magnum's growling and bared teeth, the sheer danger emanating from him like a cloud, might have finally gotten through to the man. His expression altered from anger to alarm, and then he stepped back.

"Look," he said, licking his lips, "keep that mutt under control."

"He's a highly trained attack dog," I went on smoothly. "My war dog. Right now, he's under control, but I can't guarantee anything."

Down the hall, the front door opened and slammed shut.

"Jesus," Jimmy snapped. "This isn't Grand Central Station."

He headed for the hall but halted as my father pushed past him. He took in the sight of me, Reba, Rupert, and Magnum in a single glance, his mouth a grim slash. Jimmy stood at his shoulder, rolling his eyes.

"I reckon I need to call the PD," he commented.

"If these two get frisky," I drawled lightly, "Magnum can settle them right down."

Reba stood up, glaring first at her father, then at mine.

"Get over yourselves already, dammit. Stop this *stupid* feud and understand that Dirk and I are in love. You don't have to approve, but just leave us alone."

"You can't stop this," I continued as Billy and Rupert looked at me. "Don't bother to try. If you can't shake hands and make peace for our sakes, then get the hell out of our way."

Billy drew in a deep breath. "Your mom gave me what for yesterday," he said quietly. "I've done a lot of thinking."

I silenced Magnum's growling with a quiet command. "What did you think about?"

He looked at Rupert. "At finally ending the war. Our great-grandfathers started it, but if we're men enough, maybe we can stop it."

Reba, astonished, stared at her father.

"Dad?"

Rupert turned away, his back to us, and paced to lean his hands on the counter. The tense silence ticked away, a minute, then two crawled past. What would he do? Unless he consented to at least tolerate Reba loving me, a hated Blackburn, he'd always tear her in two. She'd be forever caught between him and me.

As though he read my thoughts, he finally turned and directed his words at Reba.

"For your sake," he said quietly, "I'll be a man about this. I'll shake his hand and let you make your choice."

Laughing with excitement, Reba lunged up to embrace him.

"I love you, Dad," she cried, near tears. "I love you so much."

Ordering Magnum to stay, I, too, stood up. I held my hand out to my father.

"Dad."

He took it and pulled me into his arms.

"I don't want to lose you, son," he muttered thickly. "For your sake, and hers, I'll do my best from now on."

"I can't ask for anything more."

As our hug fest ended, Billy reached out his hand to Rupert.

"For their sake."

Rupert nodded, his left arm over Reba's shoulder.

"For their sake." He shook with my dad.

"Yahoo!" Jimmy yelled, dancing in place. "Party time, party time."

Chuckling, Billy also shook Reba's while Rupert shook mine.

"I'm sorry, Reba," he said. "I should have trusted in Dirk's good sense."

"I'm really glad to meet you at last," she replied, smiling her gorgeous smile.

"Me, too."

I took Reba from under Rupert's arm, grinning like a fool even as he and Billy eyed one another uneasily.

"I'll make this official in a more romantic setting," I said, holding both of her hands. "When I get a ring."

Reba blushed, laughing, and squeezed my fingers.

"Yeah?"

"Yeah. Reba, will you marry me?"

"You know I will, Dirk." Flinging her arms around my neck, Reba kissed me, her hands on the back of my head holding me to her. "I love you. I love you."

"I love you, m'lady." Kissing her deeply, lovingly, I half-listened to the murmured conversation nearby.

"They're trying to buy the Hopper place?" Billy asked.

"That's what I hear," Rupert replied.

"Good choice, don't you think?"

"Oh, yeah, I do. Butts up against my ranch."

"What say we give the kids a hand?" Billy went on. "We each kick in toward their down payment. As a wedding gift."

"You know, I think that's the best idea any Blackburn ever came up with."

"For a Sewell, you're smarter than you look."

To read the next book in the series type this link into your browser.
https://readerlinks.com/l/2441662

Other Books by This Author

Crossing the Line (Series)

Tempting Her CEO

Captivating the Billionaire

Heads or Tails (Series)

Her Billionaire Fixated **(Prequel)**

Her Bad Boy Obsessed

About The Author

Alyssa Lee writes short and steamy romance stories about powerful alpha men and the relatable curvy women that they fall for. She creates stories with heat, sometimes sweet and she's a total sucker for happy endings. When she is not writing she can be found relaxing with her very own forever alpha and beloved fur babies. She loves to dance and is crazy about pistachio flavored ice cream!

Free Gift

Sign up to my mailing list and receive this FREE exclusive copy of [Her Billionaire Fixated](#) (A prequel to the Heads or Tails Series). Also stay up to date with all my new releases, giveaways, contests, cover reveals and more!

To sign up to my newsletter type the following link into your browser https://bookhip.com/ZDPXQQG

Review This Book

I really hope that you have enjoyed reading this book. I absolutely love to write and it means the world to me that you chose to read my book! Could I ask a small favor? If you could take a moment to leave me a review it would be greatly appreciated!

Printed in Great Britain
by Amazon